This book belongs to

....

....

....

First published 2021 by Johnny Magory Business. Ballynafagh, Prosperous, Naas, Co. Kildare, Ireland.

ISBN: 978-1-8382152-2-4
Text, Illustrations, Design © 2021 Emma-Jane Leeson
www.JohnnyMagory.com

This book was produced entirely in Ireland (and we're really proud about that!)
Written by Emma-Jane Leeson, Kildare
Edited by Aoife Barrett, Dublin
Illustrated and Designed by Kim Shaw, Kilkenny
Printed by KPS Colour Print, Mayo

Proud Partners of CMRF Crumlin.
2% of the proceeds from the sale of this book will be donated to this charity.
Please visit www.CMRF.org for more information.

Johnny Magory
and the Farmyard Féasta

Emma-Jane Leeson

This book is dedicated to all of the amazing Little Explorers after whom the animal characters in this story are named.

As part of a competition in March 2021, they got outside and planted something before their names were randomly drawn.

Well done to you all, because of you, the world's a more beautiful place already.

Here they are.

Danny the
Irish Greyhound Pig
Name: Danny Hannigan
Age: 3
Planted: Spring Flowers

Olivia the Dexter Cow
Name: Olivia McHugh
Age: 3
Planted: Flowers

Ava the Connemara Pony
Name: Ava Spellman
Age: 9
Planted: Wild Flowers

Geordie Flynn the Galway Sheep
Name: Geordie Flynn Gary Hunt
Age: 2
Planted: Black Bean Tree

Aimee the Farmyard Hen
Name: Aimee Sophia
Coffey
Age: 5
Planted: Heathers

Shay the Stoat
Name: Shay Kelly
Age: 5
Planted: Holly Tree

Ciara the Old Irish Goat
Name: Ciara Myles
Age: 5
Planted: Ash Tree Seeds

I'll tell you a story about Johnny Magory,

His sister Lily-May and their trusty dog Ruairi.
These clever two are five and eight years old,

They're **usually** good
but they're

sometimes

bold!

Autumn or An Fómhar is a special season
in Ireland every year.

Crops in the field are fully grown and trees show off the fruit they bear.

As the duilleoga
change colour
and the temperature starts to drop,

Na feirmeoirí are busy with the harvest,
reaping their rewarding crop.

Granny and Grandad Magory live on a beautiful farm,

Set amongst the rolling green fields and full of countryside charm.

Working hard all year to provide nutritious food for everyone,

They celebrate with a giant féasta when the harvest is done.

Johnny and Lily-May **love** helping out their grandparents every year.

Everyone has special jobs to do on the farm that they love so dear.

Daddy and Grandad, with their good neighbour Jim, drive the huge tractors in the field,

Harvesting the wheat, oats and barley with the **combine**, gathering up the yield.

Mammy and Granny work hard on the feast in between their other jobs.
Soup, spuds, bacon and cabbage, all smell delicious cooking on the hobs,
With soda bread and apple tart in the range, the smells are hard to resist,

But Mammy and Granny are firm,

"Don't eat until dinner time, kids!"

they insist.

The children need to pick the torthaí from the **orchard** by the cattle guard,

Pulling on their buataisí and cotaí they head off, skipping up the yard.

Ruairí **loves** playing with his best pal Rua, the red setter farm dog,

They're **bounding** towards the orchard when out jumps a sad-looking **hog**!

Danny the Irish greyhound pig looks so glum, Ruairí and Rua ask,

"What's the matter?"

"I'm really hungry,"

Danny says.

"Grandad forgot to feed us with all the harvest clatter."

"Oh no," says Lily-May, who overhears the worrying conversation.

"Johnny, we need to feed the animals. It's an emergency situation!"

Johnny thinks it's **strange** that Grandad
would forget to feed the farmyard crew,

But as he's about to say this,
Lily-May **shouts**,

"I know what to do!"

"Let's hold a fun, farmyard

harvest feast

for everyone to enjoy right now.

We'll do the food, while Ruairi and Rua tell them,
starting with Olivia the Dexter cow !"

First, they pick some **tasty** crab apples for Ava the Connemara pony.

Some pears, plums and blackberries should stop Danny the pig from being moany.

Olivia the Dexter cow will love a bundle of **delightful** fresh cut wheat.

Some parsnips, swedes and onions would be a **treat** for Geordie Flynn the Galway sheep.

Aimee the farmyard hen is sure to **wallop up** some crunchy hazelnuts,

And Ciara the old Irish goat will gobble these tornapaí – be careful she **headbutts!**

Then Shay the **cheeky stoat** comes out from the big hawthorn tree,

To ask Lily-May if there's room for **one more** at the harvest feast.

"Of course – the more the merrier," the children answer, with a big grin.

Johnny sets the table on a fallen oak tree and says, "Let's begin."

Lily-May calls everyone to the féasta and they sit around the table.

The buzzards perch on the branches and the starlings on the electricity cable.

The ducks on the pond beside them quack-quack in angry protest,

They want some yummy brown soda bread – they only like the best.

Everyone says a big thank you to Johnny and Lily-May,

They tuck in to all the tasty bia, as Rua says

"Hurray!"

Ciara the clever goat smells Granny's apple tart and plans how to get her way.

"I would **love** to taste a real apple tart,"

she says.

"Just to mark this **special** day."

"Of course,"

says Lily-May happily, thinking the grown-ups won't mind.

She runs down the yard and **takes** the tart from behind the window blind.

They have the most **amazing feast** and share stories, jokes and rhymes.

The guests thank the children for **memories** that will last their lifetimes.

As the sun is setting the men return from the fields,
The harvest is complete and they're looking forward to their meals.

The workers gather in Granny's kitchen, thankful for the food from the land,
They eat the meal that has been prepared so lovingly by hand.

But when it's time for dessert Granny stands and **scratches her head,**

"I left that apple tart on the window sill to cool,"

she says.

"Uh Oo,"

says Lily-May starting to blush, and her heart sinks.

"We had it at our harvest feast. Tá brón orm. I didn't think."

Johnny explains about poor **hungry** Danny the pig,

"Ha! Ha!" Grandad laughs ."He really **fooled** you big!
Of course, I fed the animals, I do so every day.
They were messing with you to have some spraoi and play!"

The kitchen fills with laughter
as the children tell Grandad about their day,

"When I was your age, I believed every word those clever animals would say!"

Later, after cleaning up, they brush their teeth and climb into Granny's spare beds.

They drift away to dream land

as Granny and Grandad

place a gentle kiss

upon their heads.